TREE SOUP

A Stanley Wells Mystery

JOEL STEWART

CORGI YEARLING

TREE SOUP: A STANLEY WELLS MYSTERY
A DOUBLEDAY BOOK 978 0 440 86717 3

First published in Great Britain by Doubleday,
an imprint of Random House Children's Books
A Random House Group Company

Doubleday edition published 2008
This edition published 2011

1 3 5 7 9 10 8 6 4 2

Copyright © Joel Stewart, 2008

The Random House Group Limited supports the Forest Stewardship Council (FSC),
the leading international forest certification organization. All our titles that are printed
on Greenpeace-approved FSC-certified paper carry the FSC logo. Our paper
procurement policy can be found at www.rbooks.co.uk/environment.

Mixed Sources
Product group from well-managed
forests and other controlled sources
www.fsc.org Cert no. TT-COC-2139
© 1996 Forest Stewardship Council

Set in Cochin

Corgi Yearling Books are published by Random House Children's Books,
61–63 Uxbridge Road, London W5 5SA

Addresses for companies within The Random House Group Limited can be found at:
www.randomhouse.co.uk/offices.htm

THE RANDOM HOUSE GROUP Limited Reg. No. 954009

A CIP catalogue record for this book is available from the British Library.

Printed and bound in Great Britain by CPI Bookmarque, Croydon, CR0 4TD

For Higher Trye

Stanley Wells woke to find his private world spattered with bright morning sunlight. It lit up the old stove beside him, almost as though the thing actually worked (and wasn't just filled with straw and stones), and made a golden patchwork over the scraps of carpet and mouse-nibbled cushions that littered the caravan.

Ever since the family had moved

1

to the house in the country Stanley had worked very hard to persuade his mother to let him use the old caravan that stood, lopsided, amongst the apple trees in the orchard that lay on one side of the garden. Finally he had succeeded and now it was a place for him to escape – especially from the twins, who cried all the time in the house. He liked Cleo and Leo well enough, but it really was a lot of fuss they made, and Stanley's mother and Chris (who was the twins' father but not Stanley's) had hardly a moment for anything else.

Stanley's eyes were squinting, halfway through a yawn, when he glimpsed through his eyelashes a flash of colour at the window. There was a flapping then a swooshing sound and it reminded him of a strange whoomphing! that he had heard just as he was falling asleep the night before. In all his days living in town he'd never realized the countryside was such a noisy place! He went to the door and looked around, but couldn't make out anything that could have been the cause of the sound.

Stepping down, he picked up a freshly fallen apple from the ground and took a bite.

The air is somehow different when you can just step straight outside from where you have been sleeping. Stanley breathed it deeply for a moment. There was nothing unusual out in the orchard though, so he went back into the caravan with his apple. He munched his apple and strummed on his ukulele in turns. He was cosy and time moved slowly by in the warm, musty caravan.

Stanley's mother had checked on him every morning since he'd moved out to the garden, and as mid-morning approached he began to wonder when she would come today. Then he heard the telephone ringing faintly from the house. For a few moments he continued to strum to himself. But when the telephone didn't stop ringing, a stronger shiver of worry ran through him and he felt alone. Why was nobody answering? Why hadn't his mother come to hassle him yet?

Stanley pulled on his shoes and made his way to the house.

The telephone was still ringing as Stanley pushed at the front door, but he couldn't get into the house to answer it. The door wasn't locked. It was more as though there was something holding it shut from the other side. He leaned on it with all his weight until he finally managed to push a gap wide enough to squeeze through.

Inside he didn't recognize anything. The family had only lived there a few months and Stanley had spent some of that time staying with his father, then he'd been out in the caravan. But that wasn't why he didn't recognize the inside of the house. Up until this morning his house had not been filled with vegetation and roots. Now the whole place was alien with them, like when a potato gets left in the back of a cupboard and grows monstrous in the dark.

The telephone kept ringing and Stanley had to crawl and fight his way through the indoor undergrowth to get to it. All the time he was battling his way through, he was expecting the telephone to stop. But it rang and rang.

'Hello?' he said breathlessly into the receiver at last.

'Ah, Stanley, I was beginning to think you weren't at home,' said an impatient voice on the other end of the line.

'I wasn't. I'm staying out in the garden. I don't know where everyone else has gone . . . Sorry . . . Umm . . . Who's speaking please?' Stanley shifted his neck, trying to find a position in which to hold the telephone amongst the creepers.

'Why, Stanley, it's Doctor Moon, Doctor E. B. Moon. You'll not have forgotten me already?'

Stanley had not forgotten Dr E. B. Moon or his canine companion Morcambe, but he had not seen them since they solved the mysterious case of the wenlocks together.

'I chanced upon your father in the street only today and he gave me this number for you. My, but he's quite the conversationalist, isn't he?' Dr Moon continued.

'Yes, he doesn't get out all that much. I think he gets carried away when he does,' Stanley agreed.

'How is the new house?' asked Dr Moon. 'I hear you've moved to the countryside with your mother.'

'It's far away and countrysideish

... here and near the sea. You can see the water on two sides from the top of the garden. It was all OK until this morning, but now I can't find Mum or Chris or the twins and the house is a mess. It's as if the whole place is full of roots or something . . .' Stanley brushed one of the offending plants away from his eyes.

'Stanley, I'm on my way,' said Dr Moon. 'If you chance to see Morcambe anywhere, tell him I'll be with you soon.'

'Why? What's happened to Morcambe?' asked Stanley. But the line had already gone dead.

Stanley squeezed himself back out through the front door and went all round the outside of the house, his

feet crunching gravel in the drive then squashing grass where the garden began. How odd that Dr Moon should call just as other things were getting strange. Or maybe it wasn't so odd. He peered into each ground-floor window and saw that every room was in the same overgrown state
as the kitchen.
The car was still
parked out the
back. There was
no explanation
for what had
happened to
the house –
or to everyone
who ought to be inside.

Stanley felt something twine between his legs, and Abbie purred a bright little greeting. The cat had moved with the family to their new house but she already seemed more at home than anyone. At night, she seemed to be a part of the quiet blackness that descended here. Stanley, used to amber-coloured city nights, still found such darkness quite overwhelming and new. Now, in the morning sunlight, Abbie's fur shone warmly and Stanley lifted her up and

rubbed his face in it. She smelled of lichen and moss from the woods.

'You haven't disappeared then, too? I'm used to it from you,' he said, letting her down again because she wriggled. 'Chris always says that you like your own company.'

Abbie gave another little *prrrp* and padded over towards an opening in the undergrowth at the edge of the garden. She turned as though she was expecting Stanley to follow her, then she disappeared through the gap.

Stanley didn't know what else to do with himself so he followed Abbie along an overgrown path into the woods. He knew that the nearby stream must continue after it had run down through the garden, but he had not found the way before. This path followed the water for a short while before leaving it behind. Here there were only brambles, saplings and tiny white moths that flickered up as Stanley trod between the trees.

Where the path rejoined the stream, the woodland widened out into a small grove, and at the edge of this grove stood a wooden shack with a little veranda at the front and a neat little vegetable patch to one side. On a pole sticking up out of the roof, a piece of tattered black cloth hung limply in the dappled light. Stanley was surprised. He had no idea that there were any neighbours so close by.

Abbie went straight up to the open door of the shack, but only slipped

inside after hesitating for a moment. Stanley followed quite cautiously himself and knocked at the edge of the doorframe.

'Oh, she's like a piece o' the night, this one,' said the figure inside, reaching down to tickle Abbie. 'Even in broad daylight.' He nodded Stanley into the hut, then turned back and continued with what he was doing. Abbie's eyes followed his five heavily ringed fingers as they delicately took a tiny chip of wood from a basket on the floor, dipped it in glue and applied it to a model that was taking up the

entire table he was sitting at.

'Umm, hello. Sorry to disturb you. My name is Stanley Wells,' said Stanley. 'I live next door.'

'Jim Yarrow,' said Jim Yarrow, holding out his left hand for Stanley to shake. Stanley held out his right one automatically so the handshake was awkward and backwards.

Stanley looked past Jim at the model of a ship on the table. It was pretty much like any other model of a galleon or pirate ship you might see in a museum or on a mantelpiece, except that the twigs it was made from were rough, and the whole thing was in two pieces as though it were sinking into the sea of wooden table.

The sun flickered over the miniature scene, setting up ripples and waves

of light across the wooden ocean,
until suddenly a shadow fell across
the ship. There was a flapping at the
open window, and the large parrot that
was casting the shadow flew into the
hut to land on Jim Yarrow's shoulder.

'Ar, 'aven't ye grown,' said the
impossibly colourful bird, looking
down at the model on the table.

Abbie fled from the
shack at breakneck speed,
leaving a cloud of settling
dust and kicked-up leaves
behind her.

'She normally runs *after* birds, not away from them,' said Stanley.

'Melina's not no wren nor no robin though, now is she?' asked Jim, standing up.

Stanley saw now why he had shaken the wrong hand – because Jim's right arm was missing at the shoulder. His battered but rather complicated overcoat was tied in a knot where his arm should have been.

'Now what can I be doing for ye, young Stanley?'

'I . . . umm . . . I don't know,' said Stanley. 'I was just walking in the woods; I didn't know anybody lived here. Something's happened to my—' He stopped. He felt perhaps he shouldn't tell this strange man that he had been left alone. Jim had a glint in his eye that Stanley didn't trust.

'—to my shoe.' Stanley took off his shoe and pretended to shake a stone out of it.

'Well, me boy, I'm sure as I don't mind a little fella picking up pebbles in 'is boots and wandering about, 'ere in Melina's wood.' Jim's eyes sparkled like the jewels on his fingers as he gestured towards the trees outside the hut window. 'And sure as I don't mind a visitor neither, sitting round as I am, waiting for a delivery that should by rights 'ave arrived yesterday. Do ye know, I believe I 'aven't 'ad a visitor, but for the delivery man, since the day I washed up 'ere?' Jim took a dark old bottle from a shelf by the window then dug around in a box below the table, bringing out two heavy gold goblets whose bases were decorated with skulls.

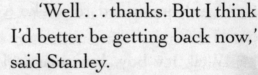

'Well ... thanks. But I think I'd better be getting back now,' said Stanley.

'Oh, 'aven't ye time for a drop?' asked Jim, moving between Stanley and the door and clinking the goblets together.

''Aven't ye . . .' said the parrot on Jim's shoulder.

'I hope your delivery shows up,' said Stanley as he slipped past them out into the woods.

Nothing had changed when Stanley got back to the house. Roots and twisty branches still pushed at the inside of every downstairs window. It would have been nice to ask someone what on earth was going on, someone who might help him look for his family, but he wasn't going to ask Jim. Stanley tried to shake the encounter out of his mind. With that dangerous glint in his eyes, Jim was just too much to worry about on top of everything else. Stanley was afraid he might melt into a puddle of question marks if he thought too hard about any of it.

He stood by the stone lion at the top of the garden in the early-afternoon shadows – very long shadows, he thought – and was suddenly and terribly hungry.

Stanley went round to the house again and pushed his way inside. After a few minutes of jungle-clearing he arrived at the kitchen table, where he found three empty bowls and a big tin of what looked like soup (it had a label with strange foreign writing on it, so he couldn't be sure). He grabbed the tin and got out again as quickly as he could manage.

Stanley took a drink from the tap outside and then he went back to the caravan, picking up another apple from the ground on the way. He put the strange foreign soup tin onto the

rickety sideboard and sat on the edge of his bed eating the apple. He pulled the blankets around himself, even though it was only early and quite warm in the caravan, and soon fell asleep. Amongst all the confusion it was really all that he could think to do.

Only a little later, Stanley woke. Wondering if Dr Moon would know to look out in the orchard for him, he wrote a note and took it round to the house to pin it to the door. Then he went back to the caravan once more, where he found Abbie curled on his bed. He joined her and was soon asleep again.

Stanley woke to a very mournful
sound and found that Abbie
was gone. Looking at his clock,
he was surprised to see that it
was morning and that despite
everything, or perhaps because
of everything, he had slept all
through yesterday afternoon
and the whole of the night.
The mournful music went

on. Stanley pulled on his clothes and grabbed his ukulele case before running out of the caravan to investigate. As he swept out he snagged his trouser leg on the door of the old stove. He stumbled and knocked the strange foreign soup tin on the sideboard and it rocked momentarily but didn't fall.

Stanley Wells found Dr E. B. Moon sitting on the stone lion playing a violin. 'Didn't you find my note?' he asked, fiddling with the tear in his trousers. 'I didn't know you played the violin.'

'Good morning, Stanley,' said Dr Moon. 'I didn't see any note, but then your house is in quite a state.' He popped his violin into its case and hopped down from the lion all in

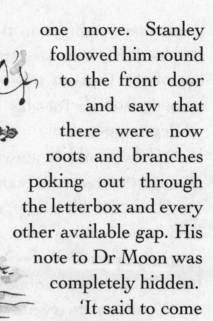

one move. Stanley followed him round to the front door and saw that there were now roots and branches poking out through the letterbox and every other available gap. His note to Dr Moon was completely hidden.

'It said to come and find me in my caravan.'

'Ah yes, you mentioned you were staying out in the garden.'

'It's good I was staying out there because . . .' Stanley nodded towards the house. 'Do you think that my mum and Chris and the twins . . . Do you think they might be in there? Maybe they're hurt. You see, the car is still here and I haven't heard anything from them since Tuesday. I don't know what's happened.'

The wind made a swishing sound through the trees and Stanley looked at Dr Moon. He bit his lip, realizing that he'd been holding back from feeling properly upset until now – perhaps only because there was nobody around.

'Dear boy, do try not to worry,' said Dr Moon. 'You know very well that if anybody can get to the bottom of a mystery then that person is me! Why, only yesterday on my way here, I was single-handedly able to return three missing zeppelins to Colonel Ballast of the Fifth Regiment. Admittedly it was a simple business since his maid had deflated them for ironing and left them clogging the laundry chute . . .'

'Where is Morcambe? I almost don't recognize you without him,' asked Stanley, blinking to clear his tear-blurred eyes. 'And where is your pipe?'

Morcambe Barnabus, long time companion of Dr E. B. Moon, was trundling, nose to ground, along the verge of a country lane. The scents all around were strong with the summer heat but he was struggling. He'd been on Dr Moon's trail now for what seemed like weeks – ever since that very grumpy policeman grabbed him in the street and carted him away. Usually it was easy to find Dr M's smoky scent. He'd never been so long without him. But it was so difficult this time, and he still wasn't sure if he was on the right track. This scent was more soapy than smoky.

Of course it didn't help that

Morcambe was so easily distracted, but he couldn't help it. He grinned and snuffled to himself as he changed direction and plunged into the undergrowth beside the lane. He had sniffed out a badger trail and now he couldn't think about anything else.

The badger trail emerged next to a broken old caravan, and here Morcambe stopped to munch a fallen apple. There was a catty smell and another smell in the air that he recognized (a dog's memory for different smells is an amazing thing). Morcambe hopped up into the caravan through the open door and went inside in search of Stanley Wells.

Dr Moon took his pipe from inside his jacket and puffed on it. A soapy bubble emerged from the bowl and drifted into the air. 'They put me away, Stanley, for smoking in a No Smoking zone, would you believe? I mean, I was outside! Now these bubbles are all I can get away with. So when I got out I took your lead with the music to give me something better to do with my hands.'

'They actually locked you up?' asked Stanley.

'Yes. For three days, four hours and seventeen minutes. I kept time by the movement of the sun and the calls of a blackbird outside the cell. It was a certain Constable Hocroft who took me in. He was in a very bad mood, even though I've given him some truly fantastic leads in the past. Since I've been free again I've not been able to find Morcambe anywhere. Usually he comes back to me quickly when we've been separated, but . . .'

Stanley was vividly imagining Dr Moon playing sad violin music to himself, all alone without Morcambe, when his thoughts were interrupted by a whooomphing sound that came from the direction of his caravan. Immediately Stanley and Dr Moon ran in the direction of the sound, and as they reached the orchard they were overtaken by a colourful blur.

'Ar, 'aven't ye grown!' called Melina the parrot as she passed above them. Then she came in to land amongst the leaves of a large tree that was now sprouting from the top of Stanley's caravan.

Stanley cupped his hands against the lichen-spotted window to peer

inside. His caravan was filled with roots, just like the house. 'But . . . how can all this stuff be growing so fast?' he said, standing back to gaze up at the roof. Then, squinting against the sunlight, he said, 'It's funny that we were just talking about Morcambe because there is something about this tree here that makes me think of him.'

'Stanley, I was just thinking the very same thing. In fact, I'll go further and say that I would know Morcambe anywhere, rogue that he is, and I am knowing him here.' Dr M pulled his soap-bubble pipe from his pocket and puffed on it furiously, sending a stream of bubbles into the air. They drifted around him, glinting, and soon he was lost in a cloud of bubbles, muttering away to himself.

'. . . I mean, there was that one case with the talking shrubbery in Frankfurt and, of course, there's many a Northland fairy tale of tree-beings —' Dr Moon's muttering was interrupted as one of his bubbles rose and burst on Melina's beak and she took off high into the air again with a squawk. She circled once or twice high above, and

41

Dr Moon began to run through the brambles below, following her.

Stanley stumbled after him, fell once or twice, tore the hole in his trouser leg even wider and . . .

'Ar, 'aven't ye grown!'

. . . was overcome with a rush of dizziness and shock. Melina the parrot was staring down at him from the branches of an even more strangely shaped group of trees that were sprouting high out of the roof of Stanley's house. Stanley had to sit on the ground to avoid falling again.

'I take it that you recognize these trees, Stanley?' asked Dr M.

'I . . . yes, I do. How could I have missed this? I just didn't look up before. Not once.'

' . . . then you have those old stories of King Hugh's time as an elm at St Cloud's under the guidance of that dreadful Djinn whatshisname . . . But, apart from the plainsmen of Yonge, who are said to turn one another into asters for not doing the washing up, it's unheard of for people, or dogs, to just go turning into trees and plants for no good reason,' said Dr Moon.

'Do you really think that's what has happened?' asked Stanley Wells, trying to pick some sense from amongst Dr Moon's waffling. 'I mean, it does look like my family up there, and they have gone missing. But could they actually have turned into trees? I feel a bit sick.'

'It doesn't seem to make sense, Stanley, but the one on top of the caravan, the Morcambe tree, it's more than just a little like him – it really feels like him. I don't know so much about these here,' said Dr Moon.

'No, that's why I feel sick, because it's the same with these. I can just tell that it is Mum and Chris and the twins,' said Stanley. 'But how? Why? And how can we change them back?' He fiddled around with his ukulele case for a moment. 'Maybe like last time?' he said suddenly, opening up the case. 'With the wenlock creatures, I mean. We just needed the right tune then.'

Stanley began to strum madly on his ukulele. Nothing happened. The trees on the roof of his house didn't shift, except for a light rustling in the leaves caused by the breeze.

Dr Moon shook his head, took his violin out and added a few half-hearted notes. 'I don't think ukulele strumming is going to solve this case the way it solved our last one, Stanley,' said Dr Moon, giving up.

'But . . . but . . . What on earth has happened?' asked Stanley. 'I mean, they've never just gone and turned into trees before. Nobody in my family

has, that I can remember. And why
Morcambe, too? Why do these kinds
of things always happen when you are
around?' Stanley sat down on the stone
lion and glared at Dr Moon.

'Well, that bird up there has a lot to
say about the trees. It's likely she has
more clues than I do.'

'You could be right about that,' said
Stanley, looking at Melina, who was

still perched in the branches.
She stared back for a few
more moments, then
flapped her wings noisily
and flew out over the
garden into the woods.
'There is someone I met
out there in the woods who
might know even more.'

They nestled their instrument cases
in the shed by the house and Stanley
led the way along the path into the
woods. When they reached the point
at which the path widened and opened
out into the grove where Jim Yarrow
kept his hut, Stanley and Dr M became
as sneaky and quiet as they could.

'The parrot belongs to the man who
lives in that hut,' whispered Stanley. 'I
spoke to him yesterday, but he worried

me and I didn't want to tell him that I'd been left alone.'

Dr M crept up to the hut and peered in through the window. He turned and beckoned to Stanley. 'There's nobody here,' he whispered.

'Yesterday he said he was waiting around for a delivery,' said Stanley, coming over to the hut.

WHOOOOOOOMPH!

From a deeper part of the woods came that noise again, and the canopy of leaves above was left shaking.

All at once, Stanley was stumbling after Dr Moon again, as he deftly and silently raced deeper into the woodland. Then, quite as suddenly, Dr Moon stopped and Stanley fell right over

him. Fortunately the noise of Stanley crashing through the undergrowth was drowned out by another whoooomph! and the swish of leaves above.

There in a smaller grove stood Jim Yarrow. He had his back to Stanley and Dr Moon, but they could see that he was leaning low to the ground, sprinkling something from a spoon over a spindly sprout of weed. Then he moved in a clockwise circle in front of the sprout.

WHOOOOOOMPH!

Now in front of Jim Yarrow suddenly stood a new and fully grown tree, its fresh green leaves jostling with the others around it in the fight for space.

'Ar, 'aven't ye grown!'
said Jim Yarrow.

Back in the orchard again, under the shadow of the Morcambe-shaped tree, Stanley flapped his arms a bit madly and puffed his cheeks in and out while stomping around amongst the fallen apples.

'Do try to calm yourself,' said Dr Moon. 'Honestly, if you don't recognize me away from Morcambe, I don't recognize you with all this panicking.

Normally you're such
a sturdy boy. And
look at the state of
your trousers! Here,
have one of these perhaps.
You must be hungry.'
Dr M picked up one
of the apples from the
ground.

'I'm sick of these apples,' said
Stanley.

'Well, I think you should eat
something. It's always important when
one is confused.'

As Dr M said this, Stanley suddenly
started trying to push his way through
the roots into the caravan.

'Whatever are you doing, Stanley?
You'll never fit in there, it's too tight.'

'There's a tin of soup stuff in there.

It's all there is apart from apples . . .'
said Stanley, slumping down in front
of the door.

'Well, let me try,' said Dr M,
climbing past him.

Moments later Dr Moon had
retrieved the tin from the caravan. He
handed it to Stanley.

But, with the tin in his hands,
Stanley continued to grow more and
more upset. He waved it about in the
air. There were bite marks in the lid,
and small puffs of dusty powder

wafted out of a gap at the edge where it was bent. 'I don't think it really is soup. I can't understand all the foreign words on the label.' He waggled the tin around even harder. 'And I can't even get the lid off.'

Just then Stanley stomped into a particularly big and rotten apple on the ground and slipped awkwardly. His hands flew back above his head and the top of the tin came off at last. At the same moment there was a swishing through the leaves of the orchard, and those of the Morcambe tree on the caravan roof.

A cloud of powder flew out of the tin, thrown by the way that Stanley had stumbled. The powder was caught by the sudden swirling breeze. It spread high and wide through the air and then fell all around like sandy rain.

'Dear, oh, dear,' said Dr Moon as he walked in a despairing clockwise circle in front of Stanley.

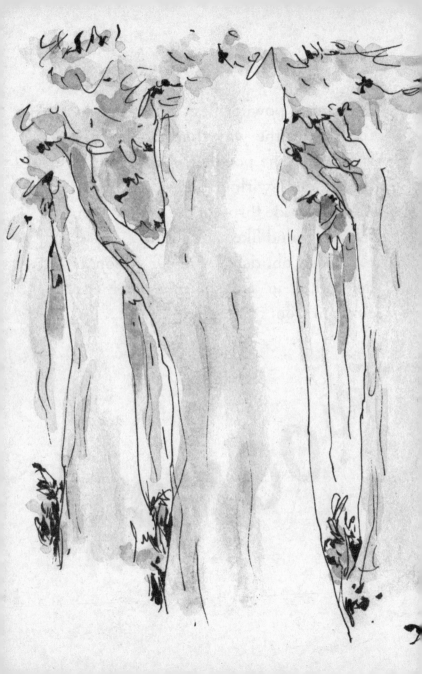

'I'm sorry I got so stroppy,' said Stanley, hugging himself. 'What do you think has happened?'

'Stanley, I am none too sure,' said Dr Moon, waving away the apology. 'But we appear to have grown ourselves a lot of extra forest.'

'Just like we saw Jim Yarrow do?'

'Jim Yarrow . . .' Dr Moon trailed off into thought.

Now that evening was descending, not much light broke through the canopy above. Stanley stopped by a broad tree trunk and sat down. 'I don't know where the house is or the caravan or anything, and I'm so hungry and tired that I . . .'

Before he had finished his own sentence Stanley had fallen into a restless, dream-filled sleep.

Dr Moon sat by him quietly for a while, blowing bubbles up into the dim. Soon, though, he was fast asleep himself.

'Stop that this instant!' shouted Dr Moon, and the shrews that were eating his ears turned into origami and rustled away across the forest floor. Peace at last, he thought to himself, grabbing a piece of the origami as it tried to escape. He unfolded it. It was a copy of the Salt Sea Gazette.

'Four-limbed Jim Yarrow . . .' said Dr Moon to himself.

The laces of Stanley's shoes creaked for a moment, then tore apart, and roots tumbled out where his toes used to be. He felt himself rising up on the vines. He felt himself growing all over. Then he was above the woods, looking down over the thin strip of land and the wide sea on either side. He'd thought, as the roots grew, that he would feel tied down. Trapped. But he bounded. They were like springs and he was bouncing over hill and moor at tremendous speed, leaving greater and greater gaps between each leap. It felt wonderful.

'Batten down the hatches, me 'earties. The old girl's ridden waves that'd make these look like ripples in a rum jug. But never with hatches that weren't both battened and down,' said Four-limbed Jim.

The crew of the Black Pike, who included: Moxley Woodnock, Rebecca Synge, Maisy Flipswitch, Norman Manners, Vernon Tuskar, Jurgen Wulfsturn, Melina the parrot and Rackstraw the ship's cat, battened the hatches double quick. And they didn't stop there. They went straight ahead and secured the mizzenmast, brushed up the coaming, whistled psalms to the taffrail and polished their deadlights. Like the fine crew they were. A fine crew, that is, in a storm.

As quick as it had arrived, the storm passed.

Four-limbed Jim paced the deck. The Narwhals were coming now, he could feel it in his famed four limbs. He grasped the rail with his two hands and peered out to sea. Turning to watch Melina flap happily amongst the rigging, he admitted to himself that the rest of his crew was at its weakest on a calm sea.

Jim Yarrow woke from his dream and blearily crossed his hut to boil a kettle for tea, or something that would help him sleep again. 'That Stanley really is the spitting image o' Vernon. Best cabin boy I ever 'ad,' he said to himself. 'Even if I did lose count o' the times I 'ad to 'ave 'im keel-hauled for getting at the rum barrel. Some moments I reckons I've gone soft as a spongefish, alone in these woods.' Jim poured a drop of rum from the old bottle into his teacup.

When Stanley woke he thought that it was still night-time. It was dark, but there was a green tinge to the darkness. When he shifted, so that the large leaf lying across his eyes fell away, he discovered that another day was well underway. He stretched back against the tree and looked round for Dr Moon. At first he didn't see him, then he was distracted by the fact that

Jim Yarrow's hut was only metres away from where they had spent the night.

Eventually Dr M stepped out from behind the hut and came towards Stanley, the morning light slipping over him as he walked. He was holding a tin in his hands and pondering deeply over the label.

'Good morning, Stanley,' he whispered. 'We'd better step further amongst the trees – Four-limbed Jim is asleep in there and we shouldn't risk waking him yet.'

'What do you mean, "Four-limbed Jim"?' asked Stanley when they had come away from the grove a little. 'Jim Yarrow's got an arm missing. It's a bit cruel to call him that, even if he is up to weird things.'

'Indeed, indeed. It's tragic,' said Dr Moon, waving a hand at Stanley but not looking up from the tin. 'But that's his name. Known throughout the seven seas – at least when I was at large on them.'

'I don't understand,' said Stanley. 'I mean, how do you know? And why would a man with a missing arm be known as Four-limbed Jim?' Stanley counted his own limbs as he said it, one, two, three, four.

'Well, one can only guess the full story . . . But you see the Jolly Roger hanging up there over Jim's shack? That's the genuine article, the flag of the most feared pirate of the last century – Four-limbed Jim. So called because he was – at least in my seafaring days when I still took the *Salt Sea Gazette* and kept up with news of that sort of thing – the only pirate on the waves to have kept his whole set,' said Dr Moon. 'Two arms, two legs and not a peg leg, hook finger or eyepatch in sight. Something must have happened to him since then. It's a high-risk career, piracy.'

'Why on earth would a famous pirate end up in a middle-of-nowhere place like this?' Stanley asked, thinking of the model of the sinking ship on Jim's table.

'Currently I am much more interested in why he has so many empty tins of your "soup" stacked round the back of his hut, and what exactly he was up to yesterday with those trees. But I suppose there's plenty of shore hereabouts, to wash up on.'

Stanley remembered his dream,

and how thin the land had seemed below him, amongst the vastness of the sea.

Dr Moon was still pondering the empty tin in his hand.

Stanley leaned over and saw that it was very similar to the one he'd spilled everywhere yesterday evening. 'Can you understand the writing?'

'No, Stanley, I can't,' said Dr Moon sheepishly. 'But look here, there are drawings.'

On the back of the tin was a series of diagrams and drawings surrounded by arrows. The diagrams were accompanied by the same foreign lettering that was on the front.

Stanley didn't even recognize the shapes of the letters, let alone the words they were spelling. 'I don't understand

the drawings either, but look there in the small print under them,' he said.

Below the drawings were printed several blocks of small text in different languages, one of which was English. It read: *In case of consumption or misuse, reverse steps and seek medical assistance.*

Stanley Wells would have considered these instructions further if Melina had not settled on his head at that moment with a very terrorizing squawk. Dr Moon, dropping the empty soup tin to the ground, waved his arms at her and tried to shoo her off. Stanley had time to be surprised by how little she weighed, before Abbie flung herself on top of the parrot from a nearby tree, and Stanley was suddenly wearing a furry, feathery, shrieking, swirling hat. The pair of them soon fell from Stanley's head in a tangle of flailing claws and paws, to wrestle briefly on

the ground before Melina freed herself from the cat and flapped raggedly up into the air and away. Abbie began to wash herself in a self-conscious, cattish way as if nothing had happened.

'Your cat is certainly very protective of you,' said Dr Moon.

'She must have followed us,' agreed Stanley, checking his face for scratches. 'But also I think she really doesn't like that parrot. Can we get even further away from here, maybe?'

Abbie led Stanley and Dr Moon back through the woods past the shed, where they collected their instruments. She did not seem fazed by the new trees at all, only wary of things that might swoop down from them.

'Apples again,' sighed Stanley when they reached the orchard. 'But I'm really too hungry to complain now.'

He started to eat one, and Dr Moon joined him.

Abbie caught something in the undergrowth and chewed on it protectively.

As they ate, Dr Moon pondered the back of Stanley's almost-empty tin, which he'd found by the caravan. 'It is the same as the ones at the back of Jim's hut,' said Dr Moon. He peered into the tin then took a sniff. 'It is not unappetizing, but it's like no soup powder I've ever smelled.'

'No, it's more of a sweet smell,' agreed Stanley, taking a sniff himself.

'Yes, not unlike the rosin I use on my violin bow.'

Stanley went to sit with Abbie under an apple tree. He strummed on his ukulele, trying to think things through.

Dr Moon started to clear a space on the ground with his feet. He kicked and scraped for a minute or so until there was an area of fresh earth, clear of leaves and twigs. He began to sketch arrows in the soil with a stick.

Stanley stopped playing and came over to look more closely at what Dr Moon was doing.

'No, no, don't stop playing, Stanley. The music may still be of some use. What's shown here on the back of the tin seems to be the dance that Jim did in the clearing yesterday.'

Stanley sat back down, baffled, and played again as he'd been told. Abbie inched out along a branch near Dr Moon and looked down at him.

Dr Moon started to dance in a clockwise circle. 'It's very simple.

I think you just make a circle like this,' he said. 'Easy enough to do by accident, even.' He opened the tin and poured a little of the mixture over a tiny sapling that was emerging near the spot he had cleared. Then he danced around the spot in another clockwise circle. But as Dr Moon came to the end of the circle, Stanley sneezed and his music jumbled. At this Dr Moon tripped forward, over the place where he had poured the soup mixture and . . .

WOOOOOOOMPH!

Dr Moon was gone, and in his place was yet *another* tall tree.

Abbie twined herself between Stanley's legs as if to comfort him, while he stared upwards to see how the new tree resembled Dr Moon. He supposed that there must be two long ear-like branches above the rest. But the tree was too tall and too mixed in amongst the others for Stanley to see from the ground. Could it have been his fault Dr Moon had turned himself into a tree like everyone else? Because of the sneeze? But surely Dr Moon shouldn't have been playing around with the strange soup powder like that?

Under the trees, Stanley felt abandoned and very small. Then he thought he heard somebody call his name from above. Abbie *miaowed* back at the voice and stared up at the tree.

Stanley hoisted himself onto the lowest branch and began to climb. It was an odd feeling, to climb a tree that was also a somebody, but he thought of the voice above and felt a strong desire to be up high. A great gust of wind shivered through the leaves and Stanley paused for a moment because he thought maybe he had heard the voice again. Climbing further, he

definitely heard his name echoing through the branches. *Is the tree calling me itself?* Stanley wondered, until there was a flailing and crashing sound amongst the branches above him.

Abbie, who had accompanied Stanley effortlessly as far as he'd climbed, shot back down again.

Stanley thought about following her, but decided to try for the next branch at least.

The branches began to shake again and suddenly Dr Moon plummeted down from the leafiest part of the tree. It was a long way down and for a split second Stanley thought that his friend would fall right past him to be dashed to pieces on the ground. But Dr M's ears, which streamed out like ribbons as he fell, caught hold of the branch above Stanley and swung him round like a trapeze artist. As suddenly as he had been falling, Dr Moon was resting on the branch as though he was quite where he always meant to be. He coughed and drew out his pipe.

'I thought this tree was you. I thought you'd changed as well,' said Stanley, slipping awkwardly and tearing his other trouser leg. He climbed breathlessly onto the same branch as Dr Moon.

'Ahem. No, Stanley, I was caught on top as it grew,' answered Dr Moon, blowing bubbles.

'Oh,' said Stanley.

Abbie crept silently out along the branch and nuzzled Dr Moon gently. He was so startled that he dropped his pipe.

Stanley watched it fall from the high branch. 'I'm sorry for making you fall over when you were dancing.'

'Not at all, Stanley,' said Dr Moon, shaking slightly. 'I should have been more careful. But you'll notice that I've uncovered the secret of the soup!'

Stanley Wells stared out across an expanse of green. From way up here in the treetop he could see just how dense the growth around his house had become, and the trees that grew out of the house above it all. 'You've not worked out the whole secret of the trees,' he told Dr Moon. 'When you put some powder on a weed and made the circle that it

shows in the diagrams, you grew a tree like magic. But it doesn't explain why anyone would turn into a tree themselves.'

'But it is a start,' said Dr Moon, making fidgety movements with his hands. 'Now can we please get down from here?'

'Yes, OK. I just wanted to see what it was like all the way up at the top,' said Stanley.

'It's green. Quite, quite green,' said Dr Moon.

'And blue,' said Stanley, looking at the expanse of sea that stretched away on either side of the land around them.

As soon as they had climbed down to ground level again Dr Moon began to pace about, still playing nervously with his hands.

Stanley sat down to try and do something about his trousers. 'If you're looking for your pipe, you dropped it in there,' he said, pointing to the soup tin. 'I saw it happen.'

Dr Moon fished his pipe out from inside the tin and was about to knock the dust from it when Stanley said, 'There was more than just the dance instructions on the back of that tin . . . Wasn't there some writing in English? It said to reverse the steps . . .'

Dr Moon raised a finger, then stepped in an anticlockwise circle, turning the little dance backwards.

Nothing happened, of course.

'It didn't work on its own the other way round either. I mean, that circle is easy enough to make by accident, like you said. Maybe if you use some of the powder again first?' Stanley suggested.

Dr M picked up the tin and shook a tiny amount onto the base of the tree he had grown, then he danced another anticlockwise circle.

And the tree they had just climbed down from was gone. It had shrunk back into itself, or the sapling it had sprouted from, as quickly as it had grown.

'As easy as that!' said Dr M, pouring fresh bubble mixture into his pipe from a small bottle.

'*Reverse the steps in case of consumption*, it said on the tin. I remember that there were bite marks and a hole in the lid, too,' said Stanley, his eyes meeting Dr Moon's.

'I might have known that eating would be key to a trouble where Morcambe Barnabus is involved,' said Dr Moon.

Dr Moon prised open a caravan window. He sprinkled some of the mixture from the tin onto the roots inside. As he did this, he puffed a great plume of bubbles into the air from his pipe – then another and another. He was excited.

The bubbles rose directly above him, out into the clear air, through the gap that was left once the tree he'd grown had shrunk again. They glinted in the sunlight and spread out across the forest, eventually bursting one by one. Neither Stanley nor Dr Moon saw it happen, but each one of these whispering little explosions caused a tiny shower of dust to be released from inside. Fine specks peppered down over the leaves of the trees below.

Dr Moon stepped back and quietly began to do his anticlockwise circle again.

Stanley had his ukulele ready, but he didn't play anything. In fact he held his breath, careful not to disturb Dr Moon, and tense with the hope that what they were trying would work.

SHHWWWEEEEEPH!

With a shrinking sound, the roots in Stanley's caravan scrunched and pulled back up through the holes in the roof where they joined with Morcambe's trunk legs, which, in that moment, weren't trunks any more. The shrinking sound seemed to Stanley as though it came from all around, as well as from his caravan.

And then there stood Morcambe, small and snuffling, in very bright

light on the edge of the caravan roof.
He gave a delighted yelp and leaped
from the caravan, bowling right into
Dr Moon and knocking him flat.
Morcambe stood on Dr M's chest, and
grinned and snorted and wagged his
tail wildly.

'Yes, hello, you,' said Dr Moon.

It made Stanley feel much better to
see them together again.

Dr Moon picked
an apple from the
ground beside him
and threw it in
the air. Sunlight
flashed across

Morcambe's fur as he jumped off Dr
Moon's chest and caught the apple in
his teeth. He munched the apple down
in one go and then chased his tail in a
happy little circle.

'He chased his tail in a clockwise
circle,' Stanley noticed.

'Indeed, just as he will have done
after eating "soup" from the tin,' said
Dr Moon.

Stanley went over to pet Morcambe
and secretly to check that he was all
normal again, that he wasn't still a little
bit treeish underneath. He wasn't. True,
his fur was pretty wiry but that was as
usual.

Abbie approached Morcambe,
sniffed at him once or twice, then
nuzzled him affectionately.

Morcambe was known to be

nervous of cats, Stanley remembered well. The dog stiffened for a moment and his hat rose on bristled fur. Then he relaxed. Shaking himself, he grinned, flashing his teeth at Abbie and then at Stanley in a way that Stanley also knew was not half so threatening as it looked. The teeth shone brightly.

Looking up, Stanley saw that it was brighter all around them now. The accidental forest had not completely disappeared, but sunlight was streaming in and there seemed many less trees than there had been a few moments before. 'Doctor! Something else has happened – look.'

Dr Moon stood up and noticed the bright light and the gaps in the forest. 'Indeed, something has!' he said. 'But what?' He pulled his pipe from his

pocket once again and puffed just a
couple of bubbles into the air.

The first bubble popped quite
quickly and Stanley saw a little shower
of dust fall from the place it had burst.
The other bubble rose higher. Stanley
craned his neck and saw it pass above
a tree nearby just as it finally popped.

'Do the anticlockwise circle again,
Doctor,' said Stanley. 'Watch that tree
there.'

Dr Moon made a mistrusting
expression with his ears, but he did

what Stanley had told him to and . . .

SHHWWEEEEE PH!

The tree that Stanley had pointed out was gone, leaving a trio of small birds flapping above it in confusion.

Dr Moon looked perplexed.

'You've got dust in your pipe,' said Stanley.

'I've what?'

'You didn't clean the tree powder out of your pipe after it fell into the tin. You've been blowing it up into the air with your bubbles. That's what happened to that tree. It was all sprinkled with powder, so when you did the dance it came down like Morcambe and all the other ones.'

Dr Moon flattened his ears back and shuffled his feet. He looked doubtful, but he blew another stream of bubbles into the air and squinted after them as they drifted and spread out. He couldn't see how far all of them got before they burst, but after a few moments he made another circle and many more of the trees from yesterday's spillage disappeared. Now the garden was almost the way that Stanley knew it from before, with mostly just apple trees remaining.

'But look, Mum and Chris and the twins are still up there,' said Stanley.

Dr Moon wet his finger and held it up to check the breeze. 'That they are is a mere matter of direction,' he said.

111

'**A**r, 'aven't ye grown, 'aven't ye grown, 'aven't ye grown,' squawked Melina in a panicky way as she crashed again through the open window. She flapped round and round the inside of Jim Yarrow's hut, screeching and squawking.

''Ere now, Melina, what's got your feathers in a flap?' cried Jim, twisting his head about to follow her as she

113

flew round and round. She shot back towards the window, snapping the mast from Jim's model ship clean in two as she swooped outside again. Jim fussed over the model for a moment or two, shaking his head, then followed her outside. He couldn't for the life of him imagine what was wrong.

From the veranda Jim could see that Melina had settled high up in a tree, staring east. There she went on squawking to herself. Jim went round to the back of his hut, almost tripping on the pile of old tins that were stacked there. There was a basket at the base of the nearest and largest tree with a system of ropes attached. Jim climbed into it and began to haul himself into the air. The ropes and pulleys were arranged in such a way that he could pull himself bit by bit, with one hand, up to a vantage point. It was like the crow's nest on a ship.

Soon he was as high in the air as Melina and he drew from his coat a neat little brass telescope. He extended the spyglass and put it to his eye, peering out in the direction in which Melina's

gaze was fixed. From his lookout post, he could see a group of trees growing from the roof of Stanley Wells's house, and Stanley with the cat and a dog and some odd little fellow with long ears standing upwind of the house. The trees on the roof were very strange, but still Jim could not think why all this would panic Melina so much. Until he noticed that the little man with the ears was dancing round and round in anticlockwise circles.

'We'll have everything as it should be in a moment,' said Dr Moon, prancing about excitedly.

Stanley didn't say anything, but he ruffled Morcambe's fur and allowed himself to feel quite hopeful.

Dr Moon stood still for a minute and tested the direction of the wind again with his finger. Then he dipped his pipe into the tin of tree soup, poured in more bubble mix and blew an enormous stream of bubbles into the air. Then he blew another and another and another until the sky was sparkling. 'That should be plenty enough to hit the target,' he said as the bubbles drifted with the wind, up and over Stanley's house.

There were so many of them that they spread right across the forest on the other side too. And out there, into the thick of the bubbles, Melina rose up, flapping and pecking angrily at them. As the bubbles burst, a fine mist of dust settled all over the trees.

Dr Moon waited just a few moments longer and then hopped

into the little anticlockwise-circle dance with a flourish.

There was a very loud and scrumpling

SHHHWWWEEEEEPH!

and in the distance a little shriek followed by a clatter and a crash, then all sorts of things happened at once.

'Oh, my head,' said Stanley's mother. 'I was having the most beautiful dream. It was as if time were washing through me and I was the slowest, calmest thing – even though there were a million tiny insects living all over me. And the wind, the wind was whispering through my . . . through me. How did we get up here, Chris? And where have all the trees gone?'

'I had the same dream. Just the same,' said Chris. 'The last thing I remember is that we were trying to calm the twins with some soup. I made enough for everyone, but Stanley was out in his caravan, then I was walking the twins round the kitchen . . . I don't know why we're up here. You know I don't like heights at all. In my dream I was fine though. So tall and yet . . . rooted. How are we going to get down?'

At the very instant Chris said this, two long moon-white ears appeared below them, over the edge of the guttering, and Dr M clambered up onto the roof.

'Good afternoon to you,' he said. 'My name is Doctor E. B. Moon. I am a great friend of Stanley's.'

Stanley's mother raised her eyebrows.

'Have you come to help us down?' asked Chris, handing Cleo to Dr Moon and looking towards the edge of the roof.

'Yes. Umm . . . There's a ladder just there, I borrowed it from your shed,' replied Dr Moon, glancing uncertainly at the child in his arms. Then he shrugged and hoisted her onto his shoulders.

'And is Stanley OK?' asked Stanley's mother, handing Leo to Dr Moon too. But she had already followed Chris down the ladder before he could answer. So Dr Moon hoisted Leo onto Cleo's shoulders and twisted his ears in a clever way for them to hold. Then he hopped nimbly onto the top of the ladder, and, placing a foot on either rail, slid to the bottom without touching a single rung.

'Again!' cried the twins.

Dr Moon's ears drooped.

'Again!'

Dr Moon climbed the ladder again.

'Again!'

'Enough!' said Dr Moon after going slowly up and fast down the ladder for the sixth time. He handed the twins back to their parents.

'Stanley's certainly OK,' said Dr Moon. 'If it weren't for him, all of you, and my partner here, too, would still be stuck on rooftops waving your branches in the air.'

Stanley didn't say anything. But he held onto his mother very tightly.

'Look at the state of your trousers! You look like Robinson Crusoe,' she said. 'I'm

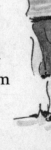

130

sorry we left you alone. I don't know what's been going on, do you? What on earth has happened to the woods?'

'Jim said they were Melina's woods,' replied Stanley. He looked out nervously towards the figure approaching across the empty stretch of land that now stood where the trees once had.

'**A**gain?' Cleo asked Dr Moon hopefully. But a moment afterwards she was distracted by the arrival of Four-limbed Jim.

'Mum, this is Jim Yarrow. He lives in the . . . in the woods next door,' said Stanley.

Jim Yarrow held out his left hand to Stanley's mother, who took hold and shook it courteously (and raised her eyebrows again). Jim looked sad and tired, and more than a little bruised. But there was still something of a sparkle in his eyes and the rings on the fingers of his one hand.

'Kraken's tail, but there's a lot o' ye!' he said. 'And I'm a mite concerned I may o' caused ye all a spot o' trouble.' He shook hands with Chris (whose eyebrows were raised, if anything, even higher than Stanley's mother's) and Dr Moon in turn. 'Sure as fish 'as fins I didn't mean no malice. You can lay to that.'

'What happened?' asked Stanley, looking at Jim's bruises. 'Have you hurt yourself?'

'Nought but a scratch. See, I was

in the treetops but a moment ago . . .
But it's me Melina 'as taken events
'ard,' said Jim.

'Who is this Melina?' asked Chris.
'And how could *you* be the cause of the
trouble we've been having?'

'You received a package a few days
ago, am I correct?' asked Dr Moon
before Jim could begin to answer. 'An
exotic-looking soup tin?'

'"Soup"? Oh, dear, dear . . .' said
Jim.

'Yes, we cooked some of it up for
the twins last night. It was so late
and they were being so difficult, all
we could do was feed them and walk
them around,' said Chris. 'I don't even
remember what the soup tasted like. I
just cooked what was to hand. I'm sure
that I meant to return the package to

the postal service, not cook it, but I was so tired.'

'I'm afraid you'll find that you served it up three nights ago. It appears that time is quite a different thing for trees. And it wasn't soup at all. That package was meant for Four-limbed . . . for Mr Yarrow here,' Dr Moon told Chris.

'It must've been misdelivered. I meant nay harm by it. Be winging from the other side o' several seas, that stuff ye be calling "soup". Old Woodnock, my boatswain, ne'er had the 'andle o' writin' out addresses.' Jim Yarrow looked from one baffled face to another and sighed. 'If ye'd all be kind enough to be following me.'

Stanley Wells and his mother, Chris, the twins, Dr Moon, Morcambe and

Abbie began to walk with Jim Yarrow out onto the blank scrubby earth that had once been the forest. They could see his lonely hut out in the distance. Its black flag fluttered in the breeze.

'Such a lot o' ye. I 'aven't 'ad such company since the deck o' the old *Pike* were shifting under me . . .' said Jim.

'Excuse me, but is it really true that you used to be a pirate?' asked Stanley.

'Aye,' replied Jim Yarrow, with

about the most wistful tone of voice that Stanley had ever heard. 'Feared o'er seven seas and more, I was. Four-limbed Jim, the blaggards called me, as yer besuited friend seems aware. Was on account o' my wondrous record o' safety amongst the rigging and skull-digging.'

'But then, how do you come to be living here in these, umm . . . these woods?' asked Stanley. Already it was hard to remember the way the land around them had been only a short while before. 'And how did you lose your arm?'

'Well now, young Stanley. A dose o' greediness is a positive boon 'mongst piratical types, and certainly were to meself once upon a time . . . Who'd 'ave known that there ought to be limits even to a pirate's greed. Yet there ought, and I ne'er should have done it. I ne'er should have took Pearl Bess's spike like I did.'

'*You took Pearl Bess's spike?*' cried Dr Moon. 'Oh, but I followed that tale in the *Salt Sea Gazette*, and I understood that the culprit was Slip-fingered Tim Bone, captain of the *Jaggy Moon*. A life sentence in Greenfinch Bay, I thought he got for it, too. I was thinking of it only days ago, in my cell . . .'

'Aye. That's as 'ow I arranged it to

appear, certainly. But then they went an' locked 'im in Gracie Mintlock's dungeon there in Greenfinch Bay, and I swears 'e whispered 'is tale to the salt wind, right through the bars,' said Jim. 'Just as I would 'ave, I do suppose, all alone there in that dank spot. The narwhals, they listened close and ye'll be spotting where that got me in the end.' He pointed the place where his right arm used to be.

'A narwhal is one of those funny whales with a twisty spike for a nose, isn't it?' asked Stanley.

'*Monodon Monoceros*, the narwhal. Infinitely proud creatures. It was a scandal before your time, Stanley,' said Dr Moon. 'The narwhals are terribly attached to those noses, and Pearl Bess's was revered amongst them all. It shone like silver and stars, so they said, and was possessed of the most perfect tapering spiral. She was a queen amongst whales. Until her spike was taken.'

'Aye. I've done my fair share o' the plundering and the thieving in this world, as you may fancy,' said Jim. 'And I'm proud to the bones for all o' it, all excepting that, though I paid for it dearly. When the narwhals came for me and Bess's glorious spike, I lost me arm, me *Black Pike* – beautiful ship that she was – and all me crew save for Melina.'

The little group had reached Jim Yarrow's hut, and there on the bare ground in front of it was Melina the parrot, pacing sadly back and forth. She took no notice of the visitors and only stared at the ground repeating the words 'Ar, 'aven't ye grown?' over and over to herself.

'Is *this* your Melina?' asked Stanley's mother. 'She seems dreadfully sad.'

'That she is. This was 'er forest, see? After I lost me *Black Pike* and me crew and all and fetched up on these shores, Melina was all I 'ad. At first I thought mayhap I'd build myself another ship. And I began to grow trees for the making o' it. But me taste for the sea was gone with me arm. Melina was ne'er so 'appy as in the rigging o' the *Black Pike*. Poor soul was 'atched in the crow's nest o' the very ship; she spent 'er life at sea. But still she stuck with me, and grew a mite fond o' the trees, as a parrot should. So I set to growin' the rest of the forest all for 'er as 'ow it might be the next best thing to a brace o' shifting masts.'

'And the *soup*?' asked Dr Moon.

'See, I'd fetched up with one tin o' something mighty special. The last loot o' all me plundering – it's legendary stuff in India and the east. An 'igh secret, used in the building o' ships, as I'd the inkling to do in the beginning. One tin I saved, but Boatswain Woodnock salvaged a deal more and 'e's sent over a tin once in a while ever since, after I wrote a-telling o' poor Melina's pining 'eart. Far away and thick as a clog though Woodnock is, 'e's a good soul (I means to say 'is soul's black as pitch – once a pirate, always a pirate – but good in its way and no less). Even this morning shows me 'e's realized 'is blunder with the address, since another package 'as been delivered.'

'And so you grew the entire woodland that used to be where we're standing, all for Melina?' asked Stanley's mother, who was becoming increasingly upset watching the parrot pacing tragically about on the blank earth.

'Aye, I was just finishing off a last little grove when I ran short.'

'But now you've more? Can't we set about replacing Melina's forest? I miss the trees myself, especially just

now,' she said.

'We could use my bubble technique!' said Dr Moon excitedly.

'If the soup-powdery bubbles were bursting above us, we might all end up trees,' warned Stanley.

Cleo began to cry and Stanley's mother sighed a little, as if she might actually quite like to end up as a tree again.

'I don't know what this bubble technique is, but I'm sure we'd all like to help in any way we can,' she said.

'Aye, but I'm with Stanley on the risks o' the bubbles,' agreed Jim, rubbing his back with his one arm. 'A little more care's in order for the choosing o' sprouting spots, in any case. But I'd be mighty obliged to ye all for a bit o' help. 'Tis a little late in the day to begin now, though, and I don't know about those as 'as been waving about in the sky, or moping along the ground.' Jim leaned his head in a gesture towards Melina. 'But I'm famished. Lend a hand, me boy, if you please?'

Jim led Stanley into the hut so fast that everyone else hardly had time to notice. A moment later, Jim's head appeared back at the door. 'One o' you landlubbers will know 'ow to pull taters, I'm sure. We'll be needing a basketful at least.' Jim waved his heavy fingers at the vegetable plot by the hut.

'I don't know as 'ow ye are making

soup from tins and all sorts o' the wrong things, but we'll 'ave something a fleet more tasty cooked up 'ere tonight,' he said, standing over Stanley at the stove. 'Me boy Vernon was the lad with the chef's touch on the *Black Pike*, but I've some tricks o' me own, and nought to do with magic powder neither. Oh, but it's a treat to 'ave an extra set o' hands stirring the pot again. Mind the rum jug though, laddie, or I'll sink ye to Davy Jones.'

Stanley and Jim stirred and chopped and sprinkled and fried, side by side, as Stanley's mother and Chris took turns to fetch a great variety of vegetables from the little plot outside.

'The stew was delicious, wasn't it?' said Stanley as he and Dr Moon walked out to the orchard in the moonlight. They had left his mother and Chris back at the house, cleaning up the potato-patch mud from the twins. No amount of joyous reunions and feasting on verandas could stand in the way of all the attention that Cleo and Leo needed.

'And Jim doesn't *seem* very dangerous for a dread pirate,' said Stanley. 'I mean, he did threaten to run each of us through with a cutlass at least once over dinner, and to have Morcambe thrown to the squid, but that's just how he talks, isn't it?'

'I doubt you can ever trust a true pirate, Stanley. But it certainly would appear that Jim's glad of the company for the moment.'

'Melina looked so sad, still. She didn't touch her stew, but just kept staring out at the empty fields.'

'Well, we'll see what we can all do about that tomorrow,' said Dr Moon. 'For now I think I'll bed down here under the apple trees. It's mild, and I found it surprisingly restful under the trees last night. I've Morcambe back for warmth now, too.' Morcambe's toothy grin flashed in the moonlight.

Stanley said goodnight to the pair of them from the steps of his caravan. He thought of joining Dr Moon and Morcambe under the apples and stars, but he found Abbie inside, already up on the bed, and they fell asleep

together. The caravan was dimly lit by the four thin moonbeams that crept in through the holes in the roof where Morcambe's tree-trunk legs had grown.

In the morning Stanley found Dr Moon throwing sticks and apples for Morcambe in the orchard. The grass was damp and the day was bright.

'Ready for a day's work, Stanley?' Dr Moon called.

Stanley wasn't, but said that he was. Abbie had followed him outside, shaking her paws free of dew at every step.

They took breakfast in the kitchen at Stanley's house, which seemed higher and wider now that it wasn't wildly overgrown inside.

'All this root damage will need fixing,' said Chris. 'I think I might

154

even get up there and work on the roof myself. I don't feel half so afraid of heights as I used to.'

After breakfast they found Jim Yarrow waiting out on his little veranda, sipping tea. 'Oh, is it fiddles ye've brung?' Jim asked Stanley and Dr M, who were carrying their instruments. 'I was a mean fiddler o' the shanties in my day, that I was. But o' course I lost that joy along with me sea legs and me arm.'

'Mine isn't a fiddle,' said Stanley, showing Jim his ukulele. 'But the doctor's is.'

'Ah, yes, yourn be one o' those jumpin' fleas such as they strum out on the islands. Oh, stir me 'eart, they all do – shanties, jigs and hulas. Ye'll play, while we lays out the trees? It'll be a

boon for the dancing.'

Jim took Melina on his shoulder and led everyone down to a spot by the stream, at the edge of the old wood. He measured a cup of tree soup each for Stanley, Dr Moon, Stanley's mother and Chris, and they got ready to set to work.

Cleo and Leo settled down on the ground to bother Morcambe and Abbie. Stanley's mother gave Morcambe a distrustful look, but he was quite good-natured about the

constant tussling and tail-pulling. It was Abbie that was less sure of the twins, but she was sticking close to Morcambe – perhaps especially because Melina was about.

Jim went first, spooning a tiny amount of the powder onto his chosen spot. 'Right then, I'll be wanting a little accompaniment for this, ceremonial like,' he said.

Stanley and Dr Moon began to play. It was dreadful. Dr M had really not been playing for long, and the

two of them had never
properly performed
together. But still,
out there on the wide
expanse of blankness, with
everyone gathered, it did
seem ceremonial.

Jim Yarrow danced
the little clockwise dance as
delicately as he could manage and . . .

woooOOOOMPH!

The first tree of Melina's new forest
shot into the sky and seemed to glow
there, with the morning light sifting
through its fresh new leaves.

Melina took flight and flew around
the perfect tree in a colourful circle.
'Ar! 'Aven't ye grown, 'aven't ye

grown!' she called over and over in a very happy tone.

'Beautiful,' said Stanley's mother, taking Stanley by the hand and whirling him round. 'But I don't think all that much of the dance.' She let go of him, and danced around the tree with Chris.

Stanley took up his strumming again and watched, amazed. He didn't know they knew how to dance.

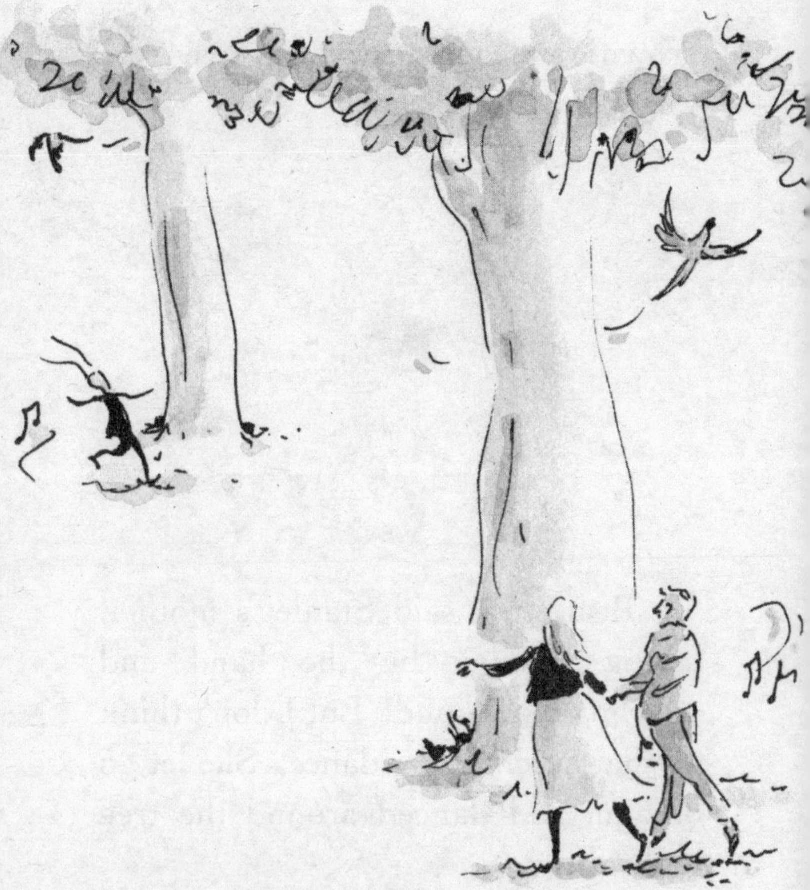

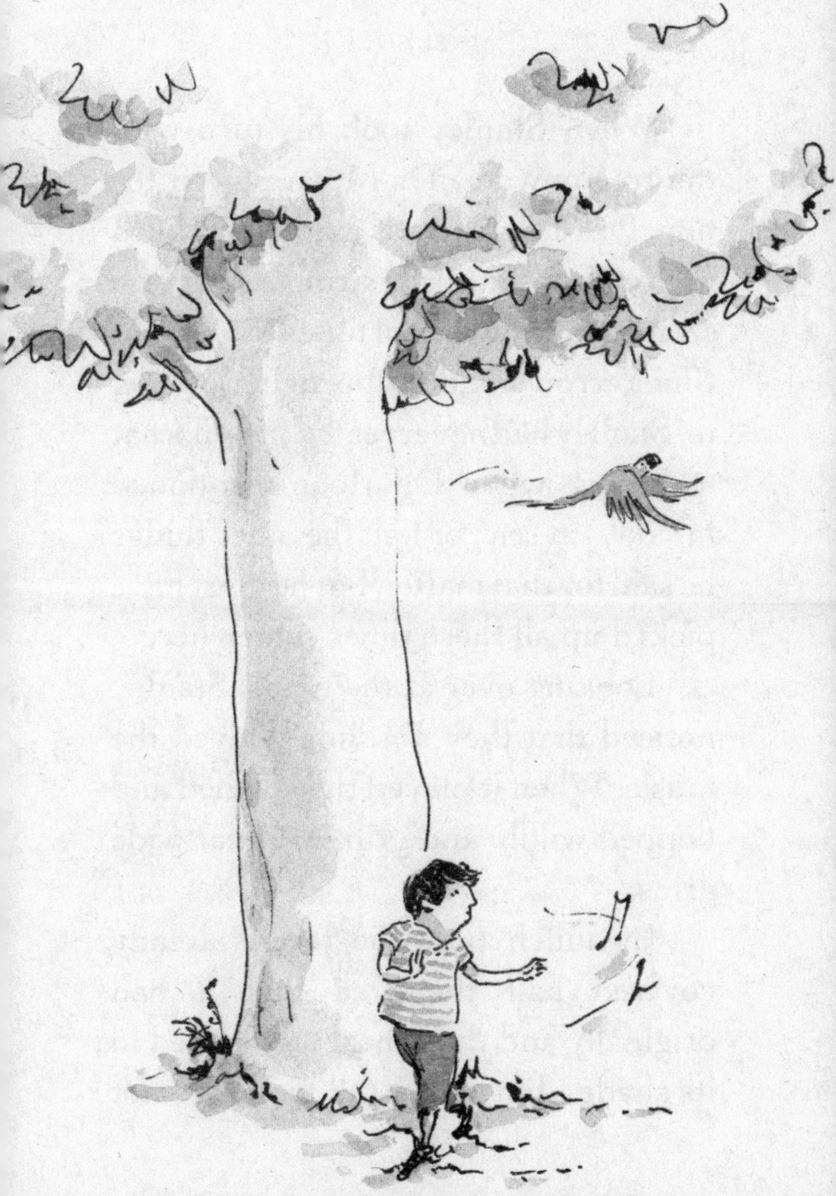

When Stanley took his turn with the tree powder, Dr Moon played for him. Dr Moon's hands might have been unpractised on his instrument, but he seemed to know a lot of tunes. Tunes that Jim Yarrow nodded approvingly along to. Stanley had never really known what to believe when Dr Moon mentioned his 'days at sea', or half the other things he said for that matter, but he must have picked up all these tunes somewhere.

Looking over at the twins, Stanley noticed that they absolutely loved the music. When it played they jiggled and bopped wildly and grinned great wide grins.

By lunch time the forest already covered half the area that it had originally and their meal was served in its shade. Jim's stew (all took care not to refer to it as soup) tasted even better than it had the previous evening. The twins enjoyed their food particularly, though Stanley wasn't sure how much of it they actually got into their mouths as they enthusiastically spooned it about. They were still waving their spoons when lunch was over.

Early evening was settling warmly as the newly grown forest neared Stanley's house. Melina flapped from tree to tree.

'Cleo and Leo are quiet,' said Chris.

'*Too* quiet,' answered Stanley's mother. 'Would you check on them, Stanley, please?'

Stanley couldn't find them. He

found only Morcambe and Abbie, asleep together, curled around the base of a comfortable tree. A nearly-empty tin of tree soup was lying nearby. Ominously, there were two spoons on the ground next to it. Stanley looked out amongst the now countless tree trunks for a while, then went to tell everybody what he thought had happened.

'Oh, no!' said Stanley's mother when she heard what he had to say. 'But if they are trees again we'll never find them amongst all these!'

'Well, I'm pretty sure that they've eaten some. The spoons are lying there, and I thought they still seemed hungry after lunch. We've done the dance nearby hundreds of times,' said Stanley.

Melina flew to Stanley's shoulder and cocked her head to one side.

'Well, we can start again in the morning,' said Dr Moon cheerily and went to dip his pipe into the tin. 'I'll have this lot down again in a jiffy.'

Melina gave a worried *squawk*.

''Old up, matey,' said Jim. 'The note from Boatswain Woodnock that arrived with the tins we've been using today said it's the last o' the lot. 'E sent a few this time, to make up for sending the last one wrong. But as I says, that's the last. I told nought before for the sake o' not worrying. But we'll not be able to bring the forest back after that tin is done and it's almost empty now.'

Melina hopped down from Stanley's shoulder and went over to the nearest tree. She sagged her head forward, clonked her beak against the bark and stayed in that position.

'It's OK. I have an idea,' said Stanley. 'What was that crazy jig you played earlier, Doctor?'

'You mean *Tin-tongued Myrtle*?' replied Dr Moon, and he played a little.

'It's nice, but it's not the one I mean. There was a really bouncy one.'

'Oh, you mean the *Whalebone Rattler*,' and he played it.

'I loves that tune,' said Jim Yarrow.

'That's the one,' said Stanley. 'Walk with me and play it, will you?'

Stanley and Dr Moon set off into the woods, playing the very lively jig. Stanley strummed chords and Dr Moon took the melody. Everyone else followed behind and the procession wove deep into the wood.

As he played and walked Stanley was watching the trees very carefully. At last Stanley saw what he was looking

for. Ahead, two trees were vigorously shaking and jiggling, far more than the light evening breeze could cause alone. He stopped playing. 'There you go. We must've lost them hours ago. We've come back very far into the forest!'

Stanley's mother and Chris looked at Stanley like they hadn't the faintest clue what he was talking about. Stanley looked back. The two trees had stopped shaking when the music stopped.

'Here,' Stanley said, taking the tree soup from Jim. Carefully, he spooned the last drops of powder onto the bases of the two trees. Then he stepped back and danced a quick anticlockwise circle.

SHHWWEEEEEPH!

Cleo and Leo, now sitting safely in their usual shapes on the ground, began to cry uncontrollably.

Stanley's mother breathed a sigh of relief. Then, as the twins went on crying, she sighed again. She liked them in their usual shapes, but did wish they could stay as quiet as trees more often.

Quickly, Stanley and Dr M struck up the music. The twins shut their mouths and began to jiggle and dance again. Then everybody danced along while Abbie led the way to Jim Yarrow's hut.

The moon rose high, casting its silver beams through the leaves of Melina's wood and shining a gentle light over the figures sitting out in the still-warm air on Jim's veranda.

'That's the last o' that then,' said Jim, putting the empty tree-soup tin to one side.

'Again!' said the twins, stretching their small hands out after it. But

Stanley's mother turned them towards
Morcambe and Abbie and they quickly
lost interest in the tin.

Out in the woods Melina could
still be heard flapping around, happily
squawking out, "Ar, 'aven't ye grown!'
every now and again.

'What with Stanley here being
the very picture of my late cabin boy
Vernon, and a taste o' 'uman company
such as I've not 'ad in years, I've 'alf
a mind to build me another ship from
all this new wood and set sail again,'
said Jim. He eyed a large two-
handled saw that he had hanging on
the outside wall of his hut. 'What say
ye, lad?'

Stanley didn't much like the idea
of becoming a 'late cabin boy' and he
liked the trees where they were, too,

especially after all that work.

'I must admit that I long to be back on the high seas, now and again,' said Dr Moon before Stanley could say anything.

Morcambe whimpered slightly and Stanley's mother shifted uneasily in her seat.

'Aye, but I reckon Melina is 'appy for now and, well, I probably don't have the strength for that kind o' caper these days anyhow,' said Jim. 'The building o' ships, nor the sailing and sinking o' them neither . . .' He went inside and returned a moment or two later, rattling a whole set of skull-encrusted goblets and waving his rum bottle. 'But if I ever does chop

these trees and weigh anchor, I'll be sure to plunder up a tin o' tree soup or two, and send ye back a package. And don't any o' ye be cooking and eating it this time!' said Jim. 'In the meantime, it sets a fresh wind blowing o'er' me 'eart to lift a drink in such fine company. Landlubbers though ye may be.' He turned and chinked his goblet against first Stanley's and then Dr Moon's.

They both raised their goblets to Jim. Stanley went to take a sip of rum, but found that his mother had quietly taken the goblet from his fingers before any could touch his lips.

Jim chinked his goblet against the ones he had handed to Stanley's mother and Chris. 'We'll 'ave to be doing this regular. All neighbourly-like!'

Stanley's mother and Chris raised

their goblets, and their eyebrows.

Stanley leaned on the rail of the veranda and looked out at the darkening wood. He didn't say anything at all.

the Whalebone Rattler

Joel Stewart was born in Barnsley and grew up in Sheffield after spending his earliest years in a commune somewhere in the wilds. He obtained a first class Honours degree in illustration from Falmouth College of Arts in Cornwall and was already working on his first picture book, *The Adventures of a Nose*, before he graduated. He knows how to play several musical instruments (including the ukulele) and draws pictures every single day (except on very rare occasions when he really, really doesn't feel like it).

Also available:
The Trouble with Wenlocks

Picture Books:
Addis Berner Bear Forgets
Dexter Bexley & the Big Blue Beastie
Dexter Bexley & the Big Blue Beastie on the Road

Other titles illustrated
by Joel Stewart:
When a Zeeder met a Xyder
Have You Ever Seen a Sneep?

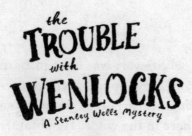

the TROUBLE with WENLOCKS

A Stanley Wells Mystery

Stanley Wells would tell you that he is an ordinary boy. It's just that sometimes extraordinary things happen around him . . .

Stanley and his unusual new friends Dr Moon and Morcambe have a mystery on their hands. There are monstrous wenlocks about, and they spell trouble. Weird things happen to the local children when they encounter these terrifying creatures. Stanley must escape from a train full of wenlocks to find out why. Can he and his companions unravel the truth, with the help of Umiko Lee and her comforting sorrow creatures? What's more, can Stanley learn to play the ukulele in the face of certain doom?

A weird and wonderful debut novel filled with fascinating characters and strange happenings, illustrated throughout with Joel Stewart's atmospheric drawings.